A KINGDOM'S VOW

HELENA SHAW

Contents

1

CHAPTER 1

The Western Kingdom of Azmariah had once been a beacon of prosperity and strength, its fields lush with harvest, its forges busy with the crafting of iron and gold.

Yet, beneath the gilded surface, the kingdom had withered under the weight of the Great War.

The once-thriving land now bore the scars of conflict and corruption, a kingdom whose heart had been poisoned by its own leaders.

Cecilia Alvarez, the Crown Princess, walked through the desolate halls of the palace, her steps echoing against the cold, empty walls.

The grandeur of the past seemed like a distant dream now, overshadowed by the grim reality of a crumbling empire.

Her engagement to Prince Leo of Rivendel was meant to be a lifeline, a way to restore hope and forge a new path for Azmariah.

But for Cecilia, it felt more like a sacrifice.

Rumors of Prince Leo's amorous escapades had reached her long before their formal engagement.

Whispers in the corridors spoke of his countless conquests, painting him as a man who pursued pleasure with little regard for consequence.

The thought of such a man becoming her husband filled Cecilia with a deep-seated disdain.

When Leo finally arrived in Azmariah, the rumors seemed to manifest before her eyes.

His demeanor was confident, bordering on arrogant, and his gaze held a hint of disinterest that stung Cecilia's pride.

The moment he met her, he made a remark that cut deeper than she could have anticipated.

"You are not a woman who can satisfy me," Leo had said, his voice laced with an edge of challenge.

Cecilia's heart had clenched at his words, interpreting them through the lens of the rumors she'd heard.

The comment only fueled her growing resentment, her imagination running wild with visions of a man who saw her as nothing more than a pawn in his game of pleasure and power.

Yet, Leo's true intentions were buried beneath layers of misunderstanding.

What he had meant to convey was far from what Cecilia assumed.

For him, the remark was not a declaration of contempt but a misguided attempt to protect her from the burdens of his past and the sacrifices his position demanded.

But Cecilia could not see this through the fog of her anger and mistrust.

As the days passed and preparations for the upcoming wedding continued, Cecilia remained distant, her thoughts preoccupied with the upcoming union.

She could not shake the feeling that she was stepping into a cage, her freedom traded for the promise of political stability.

The weight of this decision was not hers alone to bear.

The more Cecilia observed, the clearer it became how desperate her father, King Ferdinand, was for this union.

His once-sturdy frame now seemed frail under the pressure of maintaining their crumbling kingdom.

In his private chambers, he poured over treaties and correspondences, his face etched with worry lines that spoke of sleepless nights and failed negotiations.

One evening, Cecilia overheard her father's conversation with his closest advisor, Lord Hargrove, through the slightly ajar door of the council room.

"We must secure this alliance," King Ferdinand insisted, his voice tinged with desperation.

"Azmariah's very survival depends on it."

Lord Hargrove's response was measured but firm.

"Your Majesty, the people grow restless. Our coffers are nearly empty, and the nobility are becoming increasingly disillusioned.

The alliance with Rivendel is our last hope to restore stability."

Cecilia felt a pang of sympathy for her father, seeing the depth of his desperation.

But her thoughts were quickly overshadowed by the undercurrents of corruption she had witnessed within the palace walls.

The high society of Azmariah, once revered for its nobility and honor, had become a breeding ground for deceit and moral decay.

Noble families, driven by self-interest, jostled for favor and wealth, often at the expense of their own people.

The grand halls were filled with false smiles and insidious plots, where loyalty was bought and trust was a rare commodity.

Cecilia had seen enough to understand that the corruption extended beyond mere politics; it seeped into the very fabric of their society.

As she walked away from the council room, her mind was clouded with frustration.

The engagement to Prince Leo felt less like a union of hearts and more like a transaction—

a desperate bid to save a kingdom that seemed beyond repair.

Yet, beneath her growing resentment and confusion, there lay a flicker of hope.

The union with Rivendel might be the key to reversing their fate, but only if she could navigate the treacherous waters of politics and personal feelings.

Little did she know, this engagement was about to unveil truths far beyond the surface, challenging both her heart and her beliefs in ways she had never imagined.

2

CHAPTER 2

Cecilia Alvarez awoke early each morning to the gentle light filtering through her curtains.

The routine of her days had become a sanctuary from the mounting pressures of her impending marriage.

She began her day with a stroll through the palace gardens, where vibrant flowers and well-tended hedges offered a fleeting sense of peace.

The garden was her haven, a place where she could momentarily escape the weight of her duties and responsibilities.

On these tranquil mornings, Cecilia would often lose herself in the beauty of the surroundings, taking in the delicate fragrance of roses and the cheerful chirping of birds.

It was during these moments that she could almost forget the turmoil brewing beyond the palace walls.

After her garden walk, Cecilia would head to the library, a vast room lined with shelves of leather-bound volumes and ancient manuscripts.

Here, she immersed herself in literature, seeking solace in the stories of distant lands and forgotten eras.

Books provided a temporary escape from her reality, allowing her to explore worlds where she was not bound by political alliances or royal expectations.

Teatime with her friends was another cherished part of her day.

Her closest companions, Lady Eliza and Lady Marian, often joined her for these quiet gatherings.

They would sit in a sunlit parlor, sipping tea and discussing matters of little consequence—

fashion, the latest gossip, and fleeting dreams.

These moments of camaraderie were a welcome distraction from the pressures that loomed over Cecilia's life.

As the days counted down to her wedding, the palace was abuzz with activity.

Preparations for the union with Prince Leo of Rivendel consumed every corner of the estate.

The grandeur of the ceremony was to be unmatched, with elaborate decorations and a guest list that spanned the continent.

Yet, despite the spectacle, Cecilia felt increasingly detached from the celebrations.

In the final days before the wedding, Cecilia's routine remained largely unchanged, though her interactions became tinged with a sense of resignation.

She continued her walks in the garden, though now they were often accompanied by an entourage of attendants who hovered nearby, their conversations focused on the details of the wedding rather than her well-being.

The library, too, provided a familiar refuge.

Cecilia lost herself in the pages of a historical novel, her thoughts drifting to the lives of those who had lived centuries before—

people who had faced their own trials and tribulations, but whose stories had long since been resolved.

Teatime with Lady Eliza and Lady Marian took on a bitter-sweet quality.

Conversations grew more subdued as the reality of Cecilia's situation set in.

Lady Eliza, ever perceptive, noticed the strain in Cecilia's demeanor.

"You seem far away today, Cecilia," she remarked gently.

"Are you feeling unwell?"

Cecilia offered a weary smile.

"I'm just... thinking about everything that's to come. It's all rather overwhelming."

Lady Marian reached across the table, offering a comforting hand.

"We're here for you, Cecilia. Whatever happens, you're not alone in this."

Despite their reassurances, Cecilia could not shake the sense of impending change.

The palace seemed to close in around her, each moment bringing her closer to a future she had not chosen.

The final days before the wedding were filled with last-minute fittings, rehearsals, and an endless stream of formalities.

Each day blurred into the next, a whirlwind of activity that left Cecilia feeling disoriented.

On the eve of the wedding, the palace was a flurry of activity.

The grand hall was transformed into a shimmering spectacle of gold and ivory, with rows of opulent decorations and flickering candlelight.

The anticipation was palpable, yet Cecilia's heart was heavy with uncertainty.

As she prepared for the ceremony, Cecilia took one last look around her room, her gaze lingering on the familiar surroundings that had been her refuge.

With a deep breath, she steeled herself for the life that awaited her beyond the palace gates.

The next morning dawned with a sense of finality.

The grand hall, now filled with nobles and dignitaries from across the kingdoms, was a testament to the importance of the union.

Cecilia stood at the threshold, her heart racing as she prepared to walk down the aisle.

In that moment, as the first notes of the wedding march began to play, Cecilia felt a surge of conflicting emotions.

The weight of her responsibilities, the uncertainty of her future, and the fleeting hope of a new beginning all converged in a single, profound moment.

With each step she took toward her future, Cecilia knew that her life was about to change in ways she could scarcely imagine.

3

⸺ ✦ ⸺

CHAPTER 3

The grand hall of the palace was now buzzing with post-wedding festivities.

The marriage of Cecilia Alvarez and Prince Leo of Rivendel had been conducted with all the pomp and ceremony befitting royalty.

But beneath the facade of splendor, the newlyweds were already discovering the less glamorous side of their union.

In their private quarters, the atmosphere was far from serene.

Cecilia and Leo, seated across from each other at a small table, were embroiled in a heated discussion that had escalated from trivial disagreements.

"I told you, Leo, that the curtains should be blue, not green!" Cecilia said, her voice tinged with frustration.

"And I told you, Cecilia, green brings out the color of the garden!"

Leo shot back, his tone equally exasperated.

Cecilia rolled her eyes. "The garden is outside. This is our bedroom. It should be calm and neutral!"

Leo threw his hands up in mock surrender. "Neutral? It's a bedroom, not a monastery!"

Their argument continued, each trivial point of contention amplifying their irritation.

The conversation swiftly shifted to the placement of furniture.

"I think the chair should go by the window," Cecilia insisted.

"The chair is perfectly fine where it is," Leo retorted. "It's not like it's going to affect the outcome of a war."

Cecilia's eyes narrowed. "Well, if it were up to you, we'd probably be at war with the furniture."

Leo smirked, leaning back in his chair.

"And if it were up to you, we'd be having tea with the curtains."

On another fresh afternoon, Cecilia and Leo were preparing to host a diplomatic luncheon for visiting dignitaries.

As Cecilia meticulously arranged the table settings, Leo strolled in with a casual air, his gaze falling on the elaborate display.

"Do we really need this many forks?" Leo asked, picking up a silver fork with a bemused expression.

"I've never seen so many utensils in my life."

"It's for the formal dinner," Cecilia replied, trying to maintain her composure.

"Each course requires a different fork. We wouldn't want to appear uncultured."

Leo rolled his eyes dramatically. "Oh, of course. Heaven forbid we offend someone with a fork."

Cecilia shot him with a wry smile. "Well, considering you can't even remember which hand to hold your glass with, I'd say the forks are the least of our problems."

Leo's face lit up with mock indignation.

"You wound me, Cecilia. My wine-drinking habits are impeccable."

A few hours later, as they prepared to take their seats at the luncheon, Cecilia was visibly frustrated by Leo's casual approach to the proceedings.

She had meticulously planned every detail, only to find Leo nonchalantly lounging in his chair, seemingly indifferent to the formality of the event.

"Must you slouch like that?" Cecilia huffed, adjusting her posture to sit more upright.

"It's not a casual dinner at the tavern."

Leo smirked. "And must you be so stiff and proper? It's just a meal."

"Just a meal?" Cecilia echoed, her voice rising.

"This is a diplomatic event. Your lack of decorum could impact our relations."

Leo chuckled, leaning closer.

"If you insist on treating everything like a grand performance, it's no wonder you're always stressed."

Cecilia's eyes narrowed. "And if you can't take anything seriously, it's no wonder you're so frequently dismissed."

Their bickering was punctuated by exaggerated gestures and sarcastic quips, the room echoing with their playful yet pointed exchanges.

Despite their heated words, there was an undercurrent of humor and affection in their arguments—

a strange sort of bonding through their shared frustrations.

Outside their private disputes, the political landscape was far from stable.

King Ferdinand, despite his attempts to focus on his daughter's happiness, was increasingly burdened by the kingdom's dire state.

The political unrest and economic hardships had reached a critical point, and the pressure on the throne was mounting.

In the council chambers, King Ferdinand convened a meeting with his most trusted advisors, including Lord Hargrove.

"The people are growing restless," Lord Hargrove said, his voice grim.

"We're facing protests, shortages, and a collapse in morale.

The union with Rivendel was supposed to be our salvation, but it's not enough to quell the discontent."

King Ferdinand's face was lined with worry. "I can't abandon Cecilia. She's already faced so much. But if we don't find a way to stabilize the kingdom, we might lose everything."

Lord Hargrove nodded solemnly. "The nobles are more concerned with their own interests than with the welfare of the people.

They view Cecilia's marriage as a mere formality, a chance to gain favor rather than a genuine solution to our problems."

King Ferdinand's frustration was palpable. "It's disheartening. My daughter is sacrificed for the greater good, and yet those who should be allies are indifferent to her plight."

As Ferdinand grappled with his responsibilities, the high society of Azmariah remained largely disconnected from the real challenges facing the kingdom.

Social events and gossip continued unabated, with little regard for the welfare of the common people or the difficulties faced by their new princess.

During one such gathering, Cecilia overheard a conversation between two noblewomen.

"It's a shame about the princess," one woman remarked, her tone dismissive.

"But we must make do with what we have."

"Indeed," the other replied, adjusting her elaborate headdress.

"I hear she's having quite the struggle with Prince Leo. It's all very amusing, really."

Cecilia's heart sank at the casual indifference displayed by those who were supposed to be her allies.

The high society's focus on trivial matters and social maneuvering only served to underscore the isolation she felt in her new role.

As she retreated to her chambers, Cecilia reflected on the chasm between her personal struggles and the broader political turmoil.

Her arguments with Leo, though seemingly petty, were a small refuge from the larger, more daunting issues that loomed over them.

Back in the privacy of their quarters, the bickering continued, but beneath the surface, a tentative understanding was beginning to form.

Despite their disagreements, Cecilia and Leo found moments of genuine connection and even humor amidst their conflicts.

As the days passed, Cecilia came to realize that their arguments were a part of a larger journey—

a way to navigate the complexities of their relationship and the political landscape they were bound to.

4

— ◆ —

CHAPTER 4

The grand halls of Rivendel's palace were a world apart from the somber splendor of Azmariah.

As Cecilia Alvarez entered the opulent residence of her new family, she was struck by the contrast.

The palace was adorned with intricate tapestries and golden accents, a symbol of Rivendel's wealth and power.

Yet, behind the grandeur lay an air of formality that felt almost suffocating.

Cecilia was introduced to Queen Eveline and King Alistair, Leo's parents, who greeted her with polite smiles but scrutinizing eyes.

The conversation during the dinner was cordial but laced with underlying expectations.

After the initial pleasantries, Queen Eveline broached a subject that Cecilia had anticipated but hoped would be avoided for a little longer.

"It is so important for the future of our kingdoms that you and Leo provide us with an heir," Eveline said, her tone diplomatic yet firm.

"The stability of our alliance—and indeed, the prosperity of our realms—depends on the continuation of our line."

Cecilia nodded, her expression calm despite the uncomfortable nature of the request.

"I understand the importance of this, Your Majesty," she replied. "I will do my best to fulfill my duties."

Leo, however, reacted differently. His face tightened, and he abruptly cut in.

"We've just begun our life together. Can we not give us a little time before discussing such matters?"

The abruptness of Leo's response caught everyone off guard.

The tension at the table was palpable as Eveline's pleasant smile faltered.

In the days that followed, Cecilia did her best to adapt to her new life, balancing her duties with her personal sacrifices.

She accepted her role with grace, understanding the political necessity of her situation.

Despite her calm exterior, the weight of her responsibilities bore heavily on her.

Leo, on the other hand, seemed increasingly detached.

He spent long hours away from the palace, often returning at dawn with a careless air that betrayed little about where he had been.

Cecilia noticed his absences but chose not to confront him, instead focusing on her duties and the expectations placed upon her.

What Leo's parents and Cecilia did not know was that his nocturnal activities were not driven by the hedonistic pursuits of rumor but by a secret mission critical to the safety of their realms.

Leo was involved in covert operations to negotiate hidden alliances and gather intelligence that could shift the balance of power.

The secrecy surrounding his missions was paramount.

Revealing them could jeopardize not only the negotiations but also the fragile peace between the kingdoms.

Leo's reluctance to discuss his absences stemmed from a desire to protect Cecilia from the dangers and complexities of his work.

However, the lack of transparency created a rift between them.

One evening, Cecilia decided to confront Leo about the pressing issue of producing an heir.

She had been patient, but the pressure from her in-laws weighed heavily on her.

As they sat together in their private chambers, Cecilia broached the subject with forced casualness.

"Leo, I've been thinking about what Queen Eveline said," she began, her tone deliberately light.

Leo glanced up from a book, trying to appear nonchalant.

"Oh? And what did she say?"

"That we should start thinking about having a child," Cecilia said, watching his reaction carefully.

Leo shifted uncomfortably.

"Well, that's... a bit forward, don't you think?"

"Forward?" Cecilia's eyes narrowed playfully.

"We're married, Leo.

It's not exactly an outlandish request."

Leo's attempt to evade the conversation became evident as he fidgeted with his book.

"You know, there are other things we could focus on. Like—"

"Like what?" Cecilia interjected, cutting him off.

"How about whether I'm attractive enough to be a mother? Is that the problem?"

Leo looked flustered.

"What? No, that's not it at all."

Cecilia crossed her arms and tilted her head.

"So, what is it then? Am I not...

I don't know, radiant enough?"

Leo's face turned red as he struggled for words.

"It's not about you, Cecilia.

I just... need more time. Can't we just enjoy our time together?"

Cecilia raised an eyebrow, a smirk playing at her lips.

"Enjoy? Like how you enjoy sneaking out every night?"

Leo's eyes widened. "I don't sneak out! I—"

"You don't think I don't notice?" Cecilia teased, leaning closer.

"It's pretty obvious when you come back at the crack of dawn."

Leo sighed, realizing he was trapped. "Fine, fine.

But it's not because of you, Cecilia. It's complicated."

Cecilia's expression softened, but she maintained her playful tone.

"Complicated? Well, now you're making it sound like a grand adventure.

Should I start preparing for a quest?"

Leo chuckled despite himself.

"If you must know, my nights are spent on matters of state. But let's not make this about me avoiding the issue."

Cecilia sighed dramatically.

"Very well. But don't think I'm going to let this go. If I'm going to be a mother, I need you to be on board.

And you, my dear husband, need to get used to talking about it."

Leo groaned, but a smile tugged at his lips.

"Alright, alright. We'll talk about it. Just maybe not while I'm trying to escape from the clutches of politics."

Their playful bickering and laughter lightened the mood, though the underlying tensions remained.

Cecilia's willingness to confront Leo with humor and persistence contrasted sharply with his evasiveness, reflecting the complexities of their relationship and the sacrifices each was making for the greater good.

As they continued to navigate their new life together, the challenges of their marriage and the demands of their roles intertwined, shaping a future that was both uncertain and filled with potential.

5

CHAPTER 5

The grand ballroom of Rivendel's palace was abuzz with the murmurs of nobles and dignitaries, all cloaked in the finest silks and adorned with glittering jewels.

However, beneath the polished surface, the atmosphere was thick with suspicion and doubt.

Cecilia moved through the crowd, her head held high, yet she could feel the piercing eyes of Rivendel's high society upon her.

Whispers followed her like shadows, each laced with distrust.

The nobles of Rivendel were growing impatient; months had passed since the royal wedding, and still, there was no news of an heir.

It wasn't long before a prominent figure, the Duke of Avonlea, voiced what many were thinking.

"Your Grace," he addressed Cecilia during a formal dinner, "we understand the complexities of your union, but the kingdom grows anxious.

An heir would secure our alliance and solidify trust between Rivendel and Azmariah."

Cecilia, maintaining her composure, replied,

"I am aware of the concerns, my lord. These matters are not to be rushed. What is most important is the strength and unity of our kingdoms."

But the murmurs continued, as did the doubts.

There were those who began to question Cecilia's usefulness and wondered if Azmariah had other intentions behind this union.

Unbeknownst to Cecilia, these doubts were fueled by the envy and malice of a woman who had long harbored feelings for Prince Leo.

Lady Estrella of Gardiche Dukedom had always believed that she would one day become the Princess of Rivendel.

She was stunningly beautiful, with raven-black hair and eyes as sharp as a hawk's, and she carried herself with an air of entitlement that matched her station.

Her love for Leo was obsessive, a passion she had nursed since childhood.

The arrival of Cecilia shattered all her dreams.

Unable to bear the sight of Cecilia at Leo's side, Estrella's envy turned to hatred.

The rumors of Cecilia's inability to produce an heir only fed her malicious thoughts.

In her mind, Cecilia was nothing but an obstacle—

one that needed to be removed.

One evening, while Leo was preoccupied with a series of urgent meetings regarding the kingdom's defense, Estrella made her move.

She sought out a servant in the palace kitchens, a woman recently employed who was still unknown to many.

"I want you to add this to the Princess's meal," Estrella instructed, handing over a small vial filled with a clear, odorless liquid.

The servant hesitated, but Estrella's cold gaze left no room for refusal. "Do this, and your future here will be secured," she promised, her voice as sweet as poison.

Reluctantly, the servant obeyed.

That evening, Cecilia dined alone in her chambers, as Leo had been detained in yet another meeting.

The food tasted slightly off, but she dismissed it as a mere consequence of the chef's experimentation.

However, soon after finishing her meal, she began to feel light-headed.

Her vision blurred, and a wave of nausea washed over her.

Panicked, Cecilia tried to call out for help, but her voice failed her.

She collapsed onto her bed, her body growing weaker with each passing second.

Darkness closed in around her, and she lost consciousness.

When Leo finally returned to their chambers, he found Cecilia lying motionless, her skin cold and her breathing shallow.

Fear gripped his heart as he rushed to her side, shouting for the palace physicians.

In that moment, all thoughts of duty and politics vanished, replaced by a single, overwhelming emotion:

terror.

As the physicians tended to Cecilia, Leo stood by, his fists clenched, his mind racing.

How could this have happened? Who would dare harm his wife?

When the physicians confirmed that Cecilia had been poisoned, Leo's fear turned to fury.

Leo wasted no time.

He stormed into the kitchens, his expression dark and unforgiving.

The staff, who had been preparing for the next meal, froze in fear as he entered.

His voice, usually calm and composed, now thundered through the room.

"Who did this?" Leo demanded, his eyes blazing.

"Who dared poison the Princess?"

The staff looked at each other in terror, but no one spoke.

Leo's patience snapped. "If none of you confess," he growled,

"you will all pay with your lives."

The threat hung in the air like a sword over their heads.

Just as the tension reached its peak, a young servant stepped forward, trembling.

"Your Highness... it was her," she said, pointing to the woman Estrella had coerced.

The accused servant, pale and shaking, tried to deny the accusation, but the evidence was damning.

Leo ordered her to be taken to the palace's hidden chamber—a place known only to a few, where those who betrayed the crown were made to confess their sins.

The woman's pleas for mercy echoed down the corridors as she was dragged away, but Leo's heart had hardened.

Days passed, and Cecilia remained unconscious, lying in her bed as still as death.

Her beauty, even in this state, was ethereal, like a sleeping beauty from a fairy tale.

Leo could hardly bear to look at her without feeling a crushing weight of guilt and sorrow.

He spent every waking moment by her side, his duties abandoned.

His thoughts were consumed by a single goal: to find a way to save her.

He replayed the events in his mind over and over, searching for a solution, for someone who could heal her.

The palace was silent, the usual bustle subdued by the gravity of the situation.

The nobles whispered amongst themselves, wondering if Cecilia would ever wake up and what her death might mean for the alliance between Rivendel and Azmariah.

Leo ignored them all.

He refused to leave Cecilia's side, even as his advisors urged him to return to his duties.

How could he think of politics when the woman he had vowed to protect lay on the brink of death?

The days stretched into nights, and still, Cecilia did not stir.

Leo's despair deepened, but so too did his resolve.

He would not lose her—not like this.

He would find a way to wake her, no matter the cost.

As he sat beside her bed, holding her hand in his, Leo made a silent vow.

When she awoke—and she would awaken—he would be there, ready to fight for her, to protect her from all that threatened to tear them apart.

And in the depths of his heart, he knew that his life, their life together, could never be the same again.

6

CHAPTER 6

The palace was steeped in an uneasy quiet, the kind that settled after a storm had passed but before the damage could be fully assessed.

Servants moved with hushed footsteps, and the usually lively court was subdued, the nobles casting wary glances at one another.

The news of Cecilia's poisoning had spread through the kingdom like wildfire, igniting fear and suspicion.

In her chamber, Cecilia remained in her unnatural slumber, her face pale against the silken sheets.

The palace physicians had done all they could, using every known remedy, but nothing seemed to rouse her.

For days, she had been locked in that twilight state, neither truly asleep nor awake, a fragile life hanging by a thread.

Leo was a constant presence at her side, his regal composure shattered.

He had not left her room since the incident, his duties forgotten, his world narrowed to the space of her bedchamber.

The fierce prince who had commanded armies and navigated the treacherous waters of politics was now a man brought low by helplessness and fear.

It was the early hours of the morning, the time when the world was at its stillest, that Cecilia stirred.

It was just the faintest movement-

a flutter of her eyelids, a twitch of her fingers-

but to Leo, it was everything.

He sat up, his breath catching in his throat, as he watched her slowly awaken.

Cecilia's eyes opened, dazed and unfocused at first, as if she were emerging from a long, dark tunnel.

She blinked, her vision adjusting to the soft glow of the lanterns.

When her gaze finally settled on Leo, she saw the worry etched deep into his features, the relief that softened his hardened exterior.

"Leo...?" Her voice was weak, barely more than a whisper.

"I'm here," he replied, his voice thick with emotion.

He took her hand, holding it gently, as if afraid she might slip away again.

"You're safe, Cecilia. You're going to be okay."

She tried to sit up, but her body was still too weak, and she sank back into the pillows.

"What... what happened?"

"You were poisoned," Leo said, his expression darkening at the memory.

"But you're safe now. You're going to be alright."

Cecilia nodded slightly, though her mind was still hazy.

She could see the exhaustion in Leo's eyes, the toll that the past days had taken on him. "And you... have you been here the whole time?"

Leo nodded, unable to speak for a moment.

He had never imagined he would be so consumed by fear, that he would be so desperate to save her.

"I couldn't leave you. I wouldn't leave you."

As Cecilia regained her strength, the palace slowly returned to its usual rhythm, though the undercurrent of unease remained.

The attempted poisoning had shaken everyone, from the lowliest servant to the highest noble, and the search for the culprit had been relentless.

Leo, however, was no closer to discovering the true mastermind behind the attack.

The woman who had been jailed remained silent, even under the harshest interrogations.

She had confessed to nothing, revealing neither her motives nor her accomplices.

The silence only deepened the mystery and heightened Leo's frustration.

Cecilia, though still weak, was determined to help.

"We need to find out who did this," she insisted one evening as Leo sat beside her. "We can't let them get away with it."

Leo nodded grimly.

"I've tried everything, but she won't talk. Whoever is behind this is powerful, and they're determined to see you gone."

Cecilia shivered at the thought, but she refused to let fear control her.

"There must be something we can do. Someone must know something."

"There's only one person who might," Leo said, his voice heavy with reluctance. "But I'm not sure we can trust her."

"Who?" Cecilia asked, her curiosity piqued.

"Estrella of Gardiche," Leo replied, his eyes narrowing.

"She's been acting strangely since the day you fell ill. And I know she's always harbored feelings for me.

If anyone wanted to see you out of the way..."

Cecilia felt a pang of unease.

She had never paid much attention to Estrella, considering her just another member of the court, but now the pieces were starting to fall into place.

"Do you think she's capable of something like this?"

Leo sighed, running a hand through his hair.

"I don't know. But I can't ignore the possibility."

Determined to get to the bottom of the mystery, Leo and Cecilia decided to confront Estrella directly.

It was a risky move, but they were running out of options, and time was not on their side.

If Estrella was involved, they needed to uncover the truth before she could strike again.

They arranged a private meeting in the palace gardens, away from prying eyes and ears.

The setting was serene, the late afternoon sun casting a golden hue over the flowers and trees, but the tension between them was palpable.

Estrella arrived, her demeanor as cool and composed as ever, though there was a flicker of something in her eyes-nervousness, perhaps, or guilt.

"Your Highnesses," she greeted them with a respectful bow. "To what do I owe the pleasure?"

Leo wasted no time.

"We want to talk about the poisoning," he said, his tone leaving no room for pretense.

Estrella's expression remained neutral, though her eyes flicked to Cecilia for a brief moment.

"I've already told you everything I know. The entire court is concerned for the Princess's health."

"Are they?" Cecilia interjected, her voice calm but firm.

"Or are some of them more concerned with their own ambitions?"

Estrella's eyes narrowed slightly. "I'm not sure what you're implying, Your Grace."

"I think you know exactly what I'm implying," Cecilia replied, her gaze unwavering.

"There are rumors, Estrella. Rumors that you've never been pleased with my marriage to Leo.

Rumors that you might have wanted me out of the way."

For a brief moment, something dark flashed across Estrella's face, but it was quickly replaced by a mask of innocence.

"I assure you, I have no ill will toward you, Princess.

Your marriage is a union that benefits both our kingdoms."

Leo stepped forward, his patience wearing thin.

"Enough with the formalities, Estrella. If you had anything to do with the attack on Cecilia, now is the time to confess.

The woman who poisoned her is in custody, but she won't talk. If you're involved, tell us now, and maybe I can spare you."

Estrella's composure cracked, and for the first time, they saw fear in her eyes.

She opened her mouth to speak but hesitated, weighing her options. Finally, she shook her head.

"I had nothing to do with it," she said, though her voice wavered.

"Believe me, Leo, I would never harm you or your wife."

The denial did little to convince Leo or Cecilia, but without concrete proof, they were at an impasse.

Estrella's involvement remained a troubling possibility, one that would continue to haunt them as they navigated the treacherous world of court politics.

As the days passed, Cecilia slowly recovered, though the incident had left her physically and emotionally drained.

The experience had brought her and Leo closer, but it had also opened her eyes to the dangers that surrounded them.

The court was a nest of vipers, and trust was a luxury they could not afford.

Leo, for his part, was deeply affected by what had happened.

The sight of Cecilia lying helpless, poisoned by someone within their own ranks, had shaken him to his core.

He had always known the risks of his position, but he had never imagined that those risks would extend to the woman he had sworn to protect.

One night, as they sat together in their chambers, Leo spoke of his fears.

"I've spent so much time focused on the kingdom, on our alliances and enemies, that I didn't see the danger right in front of us," he admitted, his voice heavy with guilt.

"I should have been there for you, Cecilia. I should have protected you."

Cecilia reached out, taking his hand in hers.

"You can't blame yourself for this, Leo. We're both caught in a web of politics and power. But we'll get through it-together."

Her words brought him some comfort, but the burden of his responsibilities weighed heavily on his shoulders.

As they faced the uncertain future, both knew that their love would be tested in ways they could not yet imagine.

The shadows of betrayal lingered, and the path ahead was fraught with danger, but they were determined to face it side by side.

7

Chapter 7

The atmosphere between Cecilia and Leo had shifted, an unspoken tension lingering in the air since the night she had awoken from her near-death experience.

What began as a marriage of convenience, a union forged by duty and political necessity, was slowly evolving into something more complex, more tangled.

Days passed, and Cecilia found herself drawn to Leo in ways she hadn't anticipated.

There was a magnetism to him, a charm that was hard to resist, even when he infuriated her.

She could see glimpses of the man beneath the crown, beneath the mask of the prince, and those glimpses intrigued her.

Yet, every time she thought they were making progress, Leo would push her away with a jest or a teasing comment, making her question his sincerity.

One evening, as they were preparing for a formal dinner with visiting dignitaries, Cecilia stood before her mirror, adjusting the intricate braids of her hair.

Leo entered the room, already dressed in his ceremonial attire, his eyes catching her reflection in the glass.

For a moment, his gaze softened as he watched her, a flicker of something warm passing between them.

"You look lovely, Cecilia," he said, his voice unusually tender.

Cecilia's heart skipped a beat at the unexpected compliment, but she quickly masked her reaction.

"Thank you," she replied, turning to face him.

"And you look rather... princely."

He chuckled, a sound that was both endearing and exasperating.

"Is that supposed to be a compliment? I'm not sure whether to be flattered or offended."

"It was simply an observation," Cecilia retorted, though she couldn't keep the corners of her mouth from lifting into a small smile.

As they prepared to leave for the banquet, Leo reached out and took her hand, surprising her once again.

"You know, Cecilia, for all our differences, I think we make a formidable pair," he said, his tone shifting from lighthearted to sincere.

"I... appreciate your strength. More than you know."

Cecilia's breath caught in her throat, her eyes meeting his.

There was a vulnerability in his expression that she hadn't seen before, a crack in the armor he usually wore so confidently.

But before she could respond, before she could explore the emotion that had settled between them, Leo grinned and added,

"Of course, I'd appreciate it even more if you could dance without stepping on my toes tonight."

The moment shattered, and Cecilia pulled her hand away, a flicker of disappointment crossing her features.

"Perhaps if you led properly, I wouldn't need to."

Leo laughed, clearly enjoying the playful banter, but he missed the way her eyes darkened, how she turned away from him, masking her frustration.

It was these moments—these fleeting instances of sincerity, followed by a wall of humor—that made Cecilia's growing feelings for Leo so complicated.

Despite their personal struggles, the demands of the court didn't relent.

The pressure for an heir loomed over them, especially from Leo's parents and the high society of Rivendel.

Every interaction seemed to carry the weight of expectation, every glance filled with unspoken questions about when Cecilia and Leo would fulfill their duty to the kingdom.

But the conversation they had been avoiding—about bearing a child—came to a head one afternoon during a meeting with the Queen.

Cecilia had hoped to avoid the topic, but it was impossible to ignore the subtle hints and veiled comments.

"We understand that your union is still young," the Queen said, her voice calm but firm.

"But the kingdom needs stability, and an heir would secure that. You both must understand the importance of this."

Cecilia nodded, her mind racing.

She knew what was expected of her, but the thought of bringing a child into this world, into a marriage that was still so uncertain, filled her with apprehension.

"I understand, Your Majesty," she replied, choosing her words carefully.

"But perhaps a bit more time..."

Leo, who had remained silent until now, suddenly spoke up.

"We'll have a child when we're ready," he said, his tone brokering no argument. "Not a moment sooner."

His mother's eyes narrowed slightly, but she nodded.

"Of course, Leo. But do not delay too long. The kingdom is watching."

As they left the meeting, Cecilia felt the tension between them, a tension that had been simmering since the day they had first been forced into this union.

She wanted to talk about it, to understand why Leo was so resistant, but she didn't know how to approach him.

Later that evening, when they were alone, Cecilia finally gathered the courage to bring up the subject.

"Leo, about what your mother said today..."

Leo sighed, running a hand through his hair.

"I know what you're going to say, Cecilia, but I just can't do it. Not now."

"But why?" she pressed, her voice filled with both confusion and concern. "What is it that's holding you back? Is it me?

Am I not..."

Leo's head snapped up, his eyes locking onto hers. "Don't," he said sharply. "Don't think for a second that this has anything to do with you not being enough.

Because you are.

More than enough."

"Then why?" she asked, her frustration spilling over.

"Why do you keep pushing me away? Why do you make everything into a joke when all I want is for us to be honest with each other?"

Leo stared at her, his expression torn.

He opened his mouth to speak, but no words came out.

Instead, he turned away, retreating behind the walls he had built around himself. "It's complicated, Cecilia. There are things I can't explain. Things you wouldn't understand."

Cecilia felt a pang of hurt at his words, but she refused to let it show. "Maybe I would understand if you let me in, Leo. But how can I, when you keep shutting me out?"

The silence that followed was heavy, filled with all the things neither of them could say.

Finally, Leo turned back to her, his eyes softening.

"Cecilia... I'm not good at this. At being a husband, or a prince, or anything that involves other people.

But I'm trying. Please... just give me time."

Cecilia's heart ached at his plea, at the vulnerability he rarely showed.

She stepped closer, reaching out to touch his arm.

"I'm not asking for perfection, Leo. I'm just asking for you. For us to figure this out together."

For a moment, it seemed like he might let her in, that he might finally share the burden he carried.

But then, as always, he deflected with a grin.

"You know, for someone who claims not to like me, you sure spend a lot of time worrying about my feelings."

Cecilia sighed, withdrawing her hand.

"And for someone who claims not to care, you sure spend a lot of time avoiding the issue."

Leo laughed, but it was a hollow sound.

"Touché, my dear wife. Touché."

In the days that followed, the tension between them remained, though it was tempered by the slow, steady growth of their bond.

They argued often, sometimes over the smallest things—where to place a new piece of furniture, how to address certain members of the court, even what to eat for dinner.

Their arguments were passionate, but there was an undercurrent of playfulness to them, as if both were testing the boundaries of their relationship.

Leo found himself drawn to Cecilia's strength, her resilience, even as he continued to keep her at arm's length.

He admired her, respected her, and yet he couldn't bring himself to fully open up to her.

It wasn't that he didn't care—if anything, he cared too much.

But he was afraid.

Afraid of what it would mean to truly let someone in, to let her see the parts of himself he kept hidden.

Cecilia, for her part, was growing more and more frustrated with Leo's refusal to be serious.

She knew there was more to him than the carefree, teasing prince he presented to the world.

She had seen glimpses of it, in the way he had cared for her after the poisoning, in the way he looked at her when he thought she wasn't paying attention.

But every time she tried to reach out to him, he pulled away, retreating behind his jokes and deflections.

Despite this, she couldn't deny the feelings that were growing inside her.

She was beginning to care for Leo, more than she had ever thought possible.

But those feelings were complicated, tangled up in the frustration and hurt that came from his constant teasing, his refusal to be honest with her.

She wanted to understand him, to know what drove him, but he kept that part of himself locked away, out of her reach.

Their court duties continued, the demands of the kingdom pressing down on them both.

The pressure to produce an heir remained, but neither of them was ready to face that challenge.

Not yet.

There were too many unresolved issues between them, too many unspoken words.

But even as they struggled, there was a sense that something was changing between them, that the walls they had built around themselves were slowly beginning to crack.

8

Chapter 8

The pressures from both kingdoms were reaching a fever pitch.

The once-promising union between Cecilia and Leo, intended to unite two realms and bring stability, was now a focal point of tension and unrest.

Rumors of corruption and betrayal spread like wildfire, infecting every corner of the court and stirring unease among the populace.

Cecilia and Leo had been grappling with the increasing demands for an heir, but the issues went deeper than mere dissatisfaction.

Behind the facade of courtly decorum, they discovered a web of deceit that threatened to unravel everything they had worked for.

Reports of bribery, stolen funds, and treachery began to surface, revealing how deeply the corruption had embedded itself within their kingdoms.

One evening, as they pored over documents and intercepted messages, Cecilia's face grew pale with realization.

"Leo, look at this," she said, her voice trembling.

"This ledger shows transactions that can't be accounted for. And these letters... they're from a group of nobles conspiring against us."

Leo, who had been pacing the room with growing agitation, stopped in his tracks.

"This is worse than I thought. If these nobles are conspiring against us, then our marriage isn't just under threat from outside forces;

it's being undermined from within."

They exchanged worried glances, understanding that their situation was more precarious than ever.

The discovery was a double-edged sword: while it explained much of the animosity directed at them, it also highlighted their own vulnerability.

The next few days were a whirlwind of negotiations and accusations.

The pressure from both kingdoms mounted as Leo and Cecilia struggled to maintain control.

The Southern Kingdom of Rivendel was growing impatient with the lack of an heir, and the nobles of Azmariah were quick to point fingers at the royal couple, blaming them for the kingdom's deteriorating condition.

In a tense meeting with both monarchs and their advisors, Cecilia and Leo faced a barrage of criticism.

The Southern Kingdom demanded immediate assurances, while the high society of Azmariah accused Cecilia of failing in her duty.

The room was thick with tension, and the air seemed to crackle with barely restrained frustration.

"You must understand, we're doing everything we can," Leo argued, his voice strained.

"But we need time. The corruption in our courts has left us with little room to maneuver."

"That's not good enough!" one of the Southern advisors snapped. "You're expected to deliver an heir, not excuses."

Cecilia, feeling the weight of their combined scrutiny, stood up.

"Enough. We know that our marriage was intended to bring stability, but if you don't address the corruption that's poisoning both our realms, nothing we do will make a difference."

Her words were met with a stunned silence, but the dissatisfaction simmering beneath the surface was unmistakable.

The kingdoms were no longer just questioning their commitment; they were doubting their ability to rule.

Determined to address the core issue, Cecilia decided to take drastic action.

She knew that the heart of the problem lay in the corrupt practices within her father's court, and she felt compelled to confront him directly.

One evening, she requested an audience with King Ferdinand.

The old king was weary, his face lined with the burden of ruling a kingdom teetering on the edge of collapse.

Cecilia approached him with a mixture of resolve and desperation.

"Father, we need to talk," she began, her voice steady despite the turmoil within her.

"The corruption and betrayal affecting our kingdoms are severe, and it's affecting us more than you realize."

King Ferdinand looked at her, his eyes heavy with the weight of his failures.

"I know the situation is dire, Cecilia. But what do you suggest?"

"I need you to take control," Cecilia said firmly.

"You need to address the corruption within the court directly. If we don't act decisively, our kingdoms will be lost."

Ferdinand's face contorted with a mixture of anger and sadness. "You want me to take over and clean up the mess?

Do you think I don't want to?

I'm old and exhausted, Cecilia."

"I know it's a heavy burden," Cecilia said, reaching out to place a hand on his arm.

"But if we don't act now, we'll lose everything. Our marriage will be meaningless, and the kingdoms will crumble."

Her father studied her, seeing the determination in her eyes.

"Very well," he said finally, a note of resignation in his voice.

"I will do what I can. But remember, Cecilia, this isn't just about us. It's about the future of both our realms."

Cecilia nodded, a sense of grim satisfaction settling over her.

She knew the road ahead would be fraught with challenges, but she was prepared to face them head-on.

She and Leo had discovered the corruption that threatened their kingdoms, and now it was time to confront it and fight for the future they had once hoped to build.

As Cecilia and Leo prepared to face the fallout from their bold decisions, they knew that their path would not be easy.

The process of rooting out corruption and restoring trust would be a long and arduous one, filled with political intrigue and personal sacrifices.

Despite the pressures and disagreements, the challenges they faced had brought them closer in unexpected ways.

They had learned to rely on each other, to support one another through the trials that threatened to tear them apart.

Their marriage, once a mere transaction, was evolving into something more profound—

a partnership forged in the fires of adversity.

As they walked together through the palace gardens, the weight of their responsibilities hung heavy, but there was also a sense of shared purpose and renewed hope.

They knew that the road ahead would be difficult, but they were determined to face it together, to fight for their kingdoms and for the future they had yet to build.

And so, with the knowledge that they were not alone in their struggle, Cecilia and Leo braced themselves for the challenges to come, ready to confront the darkness and strive for a brighter future.

9

CHAPTER 9

The founding of the Rivendel Kingdom was an occasion of great festivity, and the royal court was alive with jubilant celebrations.

The grand hall of the Rivendel Palace was decorated with banners and garlands, and tables overflowed with lavish dishes and fine wines.

Music and laughter filled the air as nobles and dignitaries from both kingdoms mingled and toasted to the union.

Cecilia, adorned in a striking gown, tried her best to enjoy the festivities.

The evening was a rare chance to let loose, and she found herself indulging in the revelry more than usual.

As the wine flowed, her inhibitions diminished, and she laughed freely with Leo, who, like her, was embracing the celebratory mood with enthusiasm.

Leo, also significantly inebriated, was in high spirits.

His usual reservations were forgotten, and he was the life of the party, regaling guests with stories and jokes.

The two of them, caught up in the mirth of the moment, clinked glasses and danced, their laughter mingling with the music.

As the night wore on, their drunkenness grew more pronounced.

Cecilia, unable to hold her liquor, found herself leaning on Leo for support.

In their foggy state, they stumbled out of the palace together, each too tipsy to notice their blurred surroundings.

The next morning dawned with a bright sun piercing through the heavy curtains of their shared room.

Cecilia and Leo awoke to find themselves in a state of utter disarray.

Both were naked and disoriented, with no recollection of the previous night's events.

"Ugh," Cecilia groaned, her head pounding. She squinted at the unfamiliar surroundings and tried to piece together what had happened.

"What in the world...?"

Leo, equally disoriented, sat up with a confused expression.

"Did we...?" he began, but trailed off, his mind struggling to recall the events.

As they began to gather their thoughts, the situation became apparent.

Their clothes were scattered around, and the memories of the previous night were a hazy blur.

They exchanged awkward glances, trying to piece together the puzzle of their night.

"Are we... in my room or yours?" Cecilia asked, her voice tinged with both irritation and embarrassment.

"I don't even know," Leo replied, rubbing his temples.

"All I know is that I have the mother of all hangovers."

They squabbled and exchanged sarcastic remarks, each blaming the other for their current predicament.

Their hangovers only made their tempers flare more easily, resulting in a comedic exchange of grievances about the excessive drinking and the absurdity of their situation.

Despite their hangovers, Leo decided to get some fresh air and visited the stables.

The rhythmic clopping of hooves and the soothing presence of the horses provided a welcome distraction.

His servants tended to the horses while Leo paced thoughtfully, trying to make sense of the previous night.

Meanwhile, Cecilia remained in bed, nursing her headache and wishing she could just disappear.

Her thoughts were interrupted only by the occasional groan or sigh as she tried to recover from the excesses of the night before.

Leo, thinking ahead, realized that he needed to address not just the hangover but also Cecilia's safety.

The previous night's escapades had made him aware of the potential risks she faced. He decided that she needed a personal guard, someone skilled and reliable.

Leo summoned his attendants and began to consider who would be the best choice to protect Cecilia.

After some deliberation, he chose Katrina, one of his most capable female attendants.

Katrina was known not only for her skills in self-defense but also for her proficiency in various deadly arts.

Katrina was summoned to Leo's quarters, and he explained his concerns.

"I need you to become Cecilia's personal protector. Given the events of last night, I want to ensure she has someone who can handle herself and keep her safe."

Katrina, who was accustomed to dangerous assignments, nodded in understanding.

"I'll do my best, Your Highness."

With a plan in place, Leo returned to the palace, determined to face the day's challenges and ensure that Cecilia would be safe moving forward.

As he entered the palace, he couldn't help but reflect on the previous night's events with a wry smile.

Cecilia, once she managed to pull herself together, joined Leo for a quiet breakfast.

The air between them was filled with a mixture of awkwardness and newfound understanding.

Their shared experience had brought them closer in an unexpected way, and their humorous squabbles about the hangover only served to highlight their growing camaraderie.

As the day continued, the reality of their situation settled in.

They both knew that they had to address the challenges facing their kingdoms and their marriage with renewed focus.

The unexpected events of the previous night had underscored the need for them to work together and support each other in the face of adversity.

With the addition of Katrina as Cecilia's protector, they felt a sense of security that had been lacking.

The royal couple, now more aware of their responsibilities and the importance of their partnership, prepared to face the coming challenges with a renewed sense of purpose and unity.

10

CHAPTER 10

The morning sun filtered through the curtains, casting a warm glow over the royal chambers of Rivendel.

Cecilia was sitting at the vanity, brushing her long hair with measured strokes.

Leo, already dressed and ready for the day, was pacing the room with a frown, clearly annoyed about something trivial.

"Why do you always have to leave your shoes in the middle of the room?" Leo finally asked, his tone a mix of irritation and amusement.

Cecilia raised an eyebrow and glanced at the offending shoes, which were indeed lying carelessly by the bed.

"I wasn't aware I needed to adhere to your royal shoe regulations, Your Highness," she replied dryly, a smirk tugging at the corners of her lips.

Leo crossed his arms, trying to maintain a serious expression.

"It's not about regulations, Cecilia. It's about common sense. What if I trip over them in the middle of the night?"

"Then maybe you should watch where you're going," Cecilia shot back, her eyes twinkling with mischief.

"Or better yet, maybe you should stop sneaking out at night like a thief in the dark."

Leo opened his mouth to retort, but quickly closed it, realizing he was walking into a trap.

"I wasn't sneaking out," he muttered defensively.

"I had important matters to attend to."

"Of course you did," Cecilia said with exaggerated seriousness.

"And I suppose these important matters had nothing to do with the secret mission you're clearly avoiding telling me about?"

Leo blinked, caught off guard.

He hadn't expected her to notice his late-night excursions. "What makes you think I'm avoiding anything?"

Cecilia shrugged nonchalantly. "Oh, just a wild guess. You do have that suspicious look about you, you know."

Before Leo could respond, Katrina entered the room, carrying a tray of breakfast.

She set it down on the table and couldn't help but smile at the scene before her.

The Crown Princess and Prince were bickering like children, and it was a far cry from the stoic and serious faces they usually wore in public.

"Would either of you like some tea before this battle escalates any further?" Katrina asked, her tone light.

"Yes, please," Cecilia said with a grin.

"I need something to sip on while I watch him try to come up with a decent excuse."

Leo gave Katrina a mock glare. "Don't encourage her, Katrina. She's impossible enough as it is."

Katrina just laughed as she poured the tea.

"I think it's good that you're both finally acting like normal people. It makes the palace feel more... lively."

Leo and Cecilia exchanged a look, both realizing that their arguments had taken on a life of their own.

They were no longer just quarreling—

they were bonding, in a strange, roundabout way.

Their bickering had become a form of communication, a way to connect amid the pressures of royal life.

While the newlyweds found a semblance of humor in their daily lives, the Kingdom of Azmariah was crumbling under the weight of its own corruption and madness.

Rumors spread like wildfire among the nobles and commoners alike, whispering that King Ferdinand had lost his mind after marrying off his daughter to a foreign prince.

"He's gone mad, I tell you," one noble would say to another over a cup of wine.

"Ever since the marriage, he's been making irrational decisions, alienating allies, and isolating himself in his chambers."

"And to think, all this to secure a union with Rivendel," another would reply, shaking his head.

"What has it brought us? Only further ruin."

The court of Azmariah was in disarray.

Each member of the high society was more concerned with their own survival than the welfare of the kingdom.

They began to conspire against one another, seeking to seize power in the vacuum created by the king's instability.

Ferdinand, once a respected and powerful monarch, had become a shell of his former self.

His once sharp mind was clouded with paranoia, and he trusted no one—not even those closest to him.

The corruption that had slowly poisoned Azmariah now consumed it, with nobles jockeying for position and influence while the kingdom teetered on the brink of collapse.

Back in Rivendel, the atmosphere was much lighter.

Cecilia and Leo were once again at odds, this time over the proper way to arrange the pillows on the bed.

"These pillows should be fluffed, not flattened like that," Cecilia insisted, adjusting the pillows for what seemed like the hundredth time.

Leo rolled his eyes. "Who cares about pillows? They're just going to get squished when we sleep."

"That's not the point," Cecilia huffed.

"The bed should look presentable. What if someone sees it?"

"Who's going to see our bed, Cecilia?" Leo asked, barely containing his laughter. "Are you planning to host a royal tour of our bedroom?"

Katrina, who was quietly observing from the doorway, couldn't help but snicker.

The dynamic between Cecilia and Leo was something she found both amusing and endearing.

Despite their constant bickering, it was clear that they were growing closer, even if neither of them would admit it.

Cecilia threw a pillow at Leo, who dodged it with a grin.

"You're impossible," she muttered, though her tone was more playful than angry.

"And you're obsessed with pillows," Leo shot back, catching the pillow and tossing it back onto the bed.

Before the argument could escalate further, another servant entered the room, carrying a message for Leo.

He read it quickly, his expression turning serious.

"What is it?" Cecilia asked, sensing the change in his demeanor.

Leo hesitated before responding.

"News from Azmariah. It's not good. The kingdom is falling apart. The nobles are turning on each other, and your father... he's not well."

Cecilia's face fell.

Despite her frustrations with her father, she couldn't help but feel a pang of concern.

"What are we going to do?"

Leo set the message down and looked at her with determination.

"We're going to do what we must. But first, we need to put aside our squabbles and focus on the bigger picture. We need to be strong—

for both of our kingdoms."

Cecilia nodded, the gravity of the situation settling in.

Their lighthearted arguments seemed trivial now, but they also served as a reminder that they were in this together, for better or worse.

11

CHAPTER 11

In the days following the unsettling news from Azmariah, Cecilia and Leo found themselves constantly in each other's company.

What began as small, playful quarrels over trivial matters now served as a strange comfort.

Their arguments, while sometimes heated, were no longer just exchanges of sharp words but a way to connect.

Cecilia, ever the stubborn one, was growing increasingly fond of their bickering.

It was the one part of her day where she could let her guard down and be herself.

Leo, on the other hand, found joy in teasing her, knowing that it was one of the few times he could see her smile—

however fleeting it might be.

One morning, as Cecilia was rearranging the flowers on the dining table, Leo walked in with a smirk.

"Really, Cecilia? You're moving them again? I could have sworn they were fine an hour ago."

Cecilia didn't even look up from her task. "They were fine. Now they're perfect."

"Perfect?" Leo scoffed, leaning against the doorway. "You're obsessed with perfection, you know that?"

"And you're obsessed with irritating me," Cecilia retorted, finally meeting his gaze.

Her eyes sparkled with amusement despite her words.

"Maybe," Leo admitted, stepping closer. "But it's only because I know you enjoy it."

Cecilia rolled her eyes, but her lips curled into a small smile. "You're impossible."

"And yet, you're still here," Leo pointed out, his tone softer. "I must be doing something right."

As the day wore on, they continued their playful banter, each argument drawing them closer.

It was clear to both of them that something was changing, that beneath their quarrels lay a growing affection neither was ready to admit.

Meanwhile, tensions between Azmariah and Rivendel were reaching a boiling point.

The strained relations between the two kingdoms were no longer just a matter of politics—

they were a matter of survival.

Rivendel's court was in an uproar, with nobles demanding answers and solutions.

"They're making unreasonable demands," one advisor argued during a heated council meeting.

"We cannot afford to send more weapons.

Our own stores are running low."

"But we cannot abandon Azmariah entirely," another countered. "If they fall, we lose an ally."

Leo sat at the head of the table, his expression grim.

He had never wanted this marriage to be more than a political convenience, but now it was becoming something else—

something he was not prepared for.

His thoughts kept drifting back to Cecilia, to the life they were slowly building together.

The thought of her being caught in the middle of this conflict made his blood run cold.

Amidst the turmoil, Cecilia began to feel strange.

She was often tired, and the smells of certain foods suddenly made her nauseous.

At first, she dismissed it as stress from the political situation, but as the days passed, she couldn't ignore the signs.

One morning, she stood in front of the mirror, her hand resting on her stomach.

"Could it be?" she whispered to herself. The realization hit her like a tidal wave—

she was pregnant.

Cecilia knew she had to tell Leo, but something held her back.

Part of her feared how he would react, but another part feared the implications for their already fragile relationship.

Would a child bring them closer, or would it only complicate things further?

But before she could sort through her emotions, news came from Azmariah that forced her hand.

Her father, King Ferdinand, had taken a turn for the worse.

Despite the dangers, Cecilia decided to return home, hoping to reason with him and find a way to ease the tensions between their kingdoms.

The journey to Azmariah was somber, with Cecilia's mind racing the entire way.

She had once thought of Azmariah as her safe haven, a place of warmth and comfort.

But when she arrived, she found the kingdom a shadow of its former self.

Cecilia was escorted to the palace, but the moment she stepped inside, she knew something was wrong.

The air was thick with tension, and the guards' eyes were cold and unwelcoming.

Her father's throne room was dimly lit, the once-grand space now feeling more like a prison.

King Ferdinand sat on his throne, but he looked nothing like the strong ruler she remembered.

His eyes were wild, his hands trembling as he clutched the armrests.

"Father," Cecilia began, her voice trembling.

"I've come to see you, to help—"

"Help?" Ferdinand spat, his voice a harsh rasp.

"You've done nothing but betray me, Cecilia. You left us for that wretched kingdom, and now you come crawling back?"

Cecilia's heart sank.

"Father, I never wanted to leave, but it was for the good of Azmariah—"

"Good?" Ferdinand cut her off, rising unsteadily from his throne.

"You call this good? Our kingdom is falling apart, and now you dare return, expecting mercy?"

Before Cecilia could respond, the guards seized her, pulling her roughly to her knees.

"What are you doing?" she cried, struggling against their grip.

"You will stay here," Ferdinand declared, his voice cold and detached.

"You are no longer a princess of Azmariah—you are a bargaining chip. Rivendel will give us what we need, or you will suffer the consequences."

Cecilia's blood ran cold.

She was a hostage in her own home, her father's madness and desperation driving him to unimaginable cruelty.

Back in Rivendel, Leo was informed of the situation.

The message was clear—

Azmariah demanded more weapons than originally agreed upon, and if Rivendel refused, Cecilia would remain a prisoner, at the mercy of a mad king.

Leo's heart pounded in his chest as he read the letter.

His first instinct was to gather his army and march on Azmariah, to take back what was his.

But he knew that would only lead to more bloodshed.

He needed to find a way to save Cecilia without sparking a war.

But time was running out, and the stakes had never been higher.

12

CHAPTER 12

Leo's heart burned with a cold fury as he prepared to face King Ferdinand.

The letter demanding more weapons in exchange for Cecilia's freedom had pushed him to the brink.

His patience, already worn thin by the political games, snapped under the weight of Ferdinand's betrayal.

There was only one way to respond to such treachery—

by showing the might of Rivendel.

Gathering his most trusted advisors and generals, Leo laid out his plan.

"We will send a message to Azmariah, not just with words, but with action. Mobilize the troops along the border. Make sure King Ferdinand knows that if he refuses to release Cecilia, we will unleash a second Great War upon his kingdom."

The room fell silent, the gravity of Leo's command sinking in.

His advisors exchanged uneasy glances, but none dared to question him.

They all knew the stakes—

Cecilia's life, the stability of their kingdom, and the future of their alliance.

The message was sent, a stark warning of what awaited Azmariah if they continued down this path of madness.

And then, without waiting for a response, Leo personally led a detachment of elite soldiers to Azmariah, determined to bring Cecilia back.

As Leo and his men approached Azmariah's capital, the sight that greeted them was a stark contrast to the once-great kingdom.

The city was in disarray, its defenses weakened by years of internal strife and corruption.

It was clear that Azmariah was no longer the powerful kingdom it once was.

With precise, calculated movements, Leo's forces overpowered the city's guards, their resistance crumbling in the face of Rivendel's superior might.

Leo himself stormed the palace, his mind focused on one thing—

finding Cecilia.

When he finally reached her, locked away in a cold, dimly lit chamber, his heart twisted at the sight of her.

She looked pale, fragile, her once-vibrant spirit dulled by days of captivity.

But when their eyes met, he saw the flicker of defiance still burning within her.

"Leo," Cecilia whispered, her voice filled with relief and confusion.

Without a word, Leo crossed the room and pulled her into his arms, holding her tightly as if to reassure himself that she was real, that she was safe.

But the moment of reunion was brief, for they both knew the deeper conflict that lay ahead.

As they left the palace, the weight of Cecilia's decision began to settle on her shoulders.

She glanced back at the crumbling walls of her childhood home, the kingdom that had sold her for an alliance, and felt a pang of sorrow.

Azmariah had betrayed her, yet it was still the land she had once loved.

But Rivendel was no easier.

Though they had accepted her as their princess, the responsibilities that came with it were overwhelming.

She was caught between two worlds, two loyalties, and she didn't know where she truly belonged.

Leo, sensing her turmoil, remained silent as they rode back to Rivendel.

His thoughts were consumed by his growing rage at King Ferdinand, but also by the realization of how much Cecilia had sacrificed for both kingdoms.

When they finally arrived at Rivendel, Leo could hold his anger no longer.

Once inside the palace, Leo confronted Cecilia, his voice trembling with a mix of fury and concern.

"Why didn't you tell me?" he demanded, his eyes locking onto hers.

"Tell you what?" Cecilia asked, confused by his sudden outburst.

"About the child," Leo said, his tone softening as he placed a hand on her stomach.

"You're pregnant, Cecilia. And you didn't tell me."

Cecilia's breath caught in her throat.

She had suspected, but hearing it confirmed by Leo left her reeling.

"I...I didn't know for sure," she stammered. "And with everything that's happened, I—"

"You shouldn't have been forced to go back to that madman's kingdom," Leo interrupted, his anger flaring up again.

"Your father is a mad king, and he nearly cost us everything."

Cecilia looked away, unable to meet his gaze.

She had known her father was unstable, but hearing Leo call him mad was a harsh reminder of how far Azmariah had fallen.

Meanwhile, back in Azmariah, King Ferdinand received the news of Rivendel's advance with a mix of fear and defiance.

His kingdom was crumbling, his power slipping through his fingers, but he refused to back down.

The thought of surrendering to Rivendel was unbearable, yet the reality of his situation was inescapable.

Leo's threat of war was not an empty one. Azmariah was at the mercy of Rivendel, and Ferdinand knew it.

His advisors urged him to capitulate, to save what little remained of their kingdom, but Ferdinand's pride held him back.

In the end, it was not Leo's soldiers or even his threats that broke Ferdinand's resolve—

it was the knowledge that his own daughter had been caught in the crossfire of his madness.

The realization that he had nearly sacrificed Cecilia, the one person he had once sworn to protect, was too much for him to bear.

Azmariah's court, once filled with ambitious nobles and scheming politicians, was now a shadow of its former self.

The kingdom was in ruins, and its king, once a formidable ruler, was reduced to a broken man.

Back in Rivendel, Leo and Cecilia faced a new challenge—

rebuilding what had been broken, not just in their kingdoms, but in their own hearts.

The road ahead was uncertain, and the stakes were higher than ever.

But they were no longer alone.

For the first time, they were united, not just by duty or circumstance, but by something deeper—

something that would carry them through whatever came next.

13

— ◆ —

CHAPTER 13

The news of Cecilia's pregnancy spread quickly through the halls of Rivendel, a ripple of excitement and anxiety in equal measure.

The future heir to both Azmariah and Rivendel was now more than just a hope-

it was a reality.

The pressure on Cecilia and Leo had never been greater, and the entire kingdom was abuzz with anticipation.

Cecilia sat by the window in their chambers, her hand resting gently on her slightly rounded belly.

She could feel the weight of expectation from all sides-both her homeland of Azmariah and her new home in Rivendel.

It was as if the future of both kingdoms was resting on her shoulders, and it was a burden she couldn't escape.

Leo entered the room, his expression unreadable as he approached her.

He had been quieter than usual since learning of her pregnancy, his moods shifting unpredictably as he wrestled with the responsibilities and fears that came with impending fatherhood.

"Everyone is talking about the baby," Cecilia said softly, not looking up from the view outside.

"The advisors, the servants, the nobles-

they all have their own opinions about what this child means for our kingdoms."

Leo sighed, running a hand through his hair as he joined her by the window.

"It's not just about the baby, Cecilia. It's about everything-our marriage, our alliances, our future. Everyone's expectations are suffocating us, and it's only going to get worse."

Cecilia nodded, understanding his frustration. "I know. But we have to focus on what's important-protecting our child, securing peace between our kingdoms. We can't let the pressure break us."

Leo's eyes softened as he looked at her, his hand resting on hers.

"You're right. We have to stay strong, for the baby's sake.

But it's hard to focus on peace when war is knocking at our door."

The situation in Azmariah had grown more dire by the day.

King Ferdinand's erratic behavior had escalated, and rumors of his madness spread like wildfire.

The kingdom was teetering on the brink of chaos, with nobles and commoners alike questioning his ability to rule.

When news of Cecilia's pregnancy reached Azmariah, it should have been a cause for celebration, a symbol of hope and renewal.

Instead, it only deepened the rift between the two kingdoms.

For King Ferdinand, the child represented a loss of control, a threat to his authority.

He saw the future heir as a pawn in Rivendel's hands, a symbol of his kingdom's submission.

Desperate to assert his dominance, King Ferdinand made outrageous demands, insisting that Rivendel provide more weapons and resources than originally agreed upon in their marriage alliance.

He threatened war, using Cecilia's safety as leverage to force Rivendel's hand.

Cecilia was horrified when she learned of her father's ultimatum.

The man she had once looked up to as a pillar of strength and wisdom was now little more than a tyrant, driven by political mania and desperation.

She knew that returning to Azmariah, even to negotiate, would be a dangerous move, but she couldn't stand by and watch her father destroy everything she cared about.

"I have to go to him," Cecilia told Leo one evening, her voice steady but filled with determination.

"I have to try and talk sense into him before this escalates any further. If he truly cares about me and our child, he'll listen."

Leo's expression darkened with concern.

"Cecilia, you know how unstable your father has become. What if he uses you as a bargaining chip?

What if he tries to keep you there, or worse?"

"I have to try," Cecilia insisted. "This is my responsibility, Leo. I won't let our child be born into a world at war, not if I can do something to stop it."

Leo's gaze softened, seeing the fierce resolve in her eyes.

He knew there was no stopping her once she had made up her mind.

"If you go, then I'm coming with you. I won't let you face him alone."

Cecilia nodded, relieved that he would be by her side.

They would face this together, no matter how difficult the road ahead might be.

The journey to Azmariah was tense, filled with uncertainty.

As they arrived at the palace, the atmosphere was thick with unease.

The once-grand halls now seemed like a prison, the walls closing in as they made their way to the throne room.

King Ferdinand sat on his throne, a twisted smile on his face as he saw his daughter enter.

"Cecilia, my dear," he crooned, his tone dripping with false warmth.

"You've returned home. And I see you've brought the prince with you. How...predictable."

Cecilia stood tall, refusing to be intimidated by the man who had once been her protector.

"Father, this has to stop," she said firmly.

"These demands, these threats-they're tearing our kingdoms apart.

Think of the future, of your grandchild.

Don't let your pride destroy everything."

Ferdinand's smile faded, his eyes narrowing with suspicion.

"You think I'm the one destroying everything? It's Rivendel that seeks to strip Azmariah of its power, of its rightful place.

You think you've secured peace with this marriage, but all you've done is hand our kingdom over to our enemies."

Leo stepped forward, his voice cold and authoritative. "You are a paranoid old man, Ferdinand. This alliance was meant to strengthen both our kingdoms, not weaken them.

If you continue down this path, you'll leave Azmariah in ruins."

King Ferdinand's eyes flicked to Leo, a dangerous glint in them.

"And what will you do, Prince of Rivendel? Start a war to take what's left of Azmariah?

You forget, my daughter is still of this kingdom, and so is her child."

Cecilia's heart pounded in her chest, the tension thick enough to cut with a knife.

She knew Leo was struggling to keep his composure, his protective instincts battling with his desire to avoid conflict.

But then Leo spoke, his voice steady and unwavering.

"I've given you every chance to make peace, Ferdinand. But if you threaten my family, my child, then know this-

I will not hesitate to protect them by any means necessary.

If that means war, then so be it."

The words hung in the air, a stark reminder of the stakes at play.

Cecilia saw the flicker of fear in her father's eyes, a brief moment of clarity in the midst of his madness.

He realized that he had pushed too far, that the threat of war was not an empty one.

King Ferdinand's gaze dropped, the fight draining from him as he slumped back in his throne.

"Take her," he muttered, his voice a mere whisper.

"Take her and go. But remember this, Leo-Azmariah will never forget this betrayal."

Cecilia felt a pang of sorrow as she looked at her father, a man consumed by his own fears.

But she knew there was no turning back now.

She took Leo's hand, and together they left the palace, the weight of their decision heavy on their hearts.

As they boarded the carriage back to Rivendel, Cecilia leaned into Leo, exhaustion and relief washing over her.

"Thank you," she whispered, her hand resting on her belly. "For everything."

Leo wrapped an arm around her, pressing a kiss to her forehead.

"We'll get through this, Cecilia. Together."

And as they traveled back to Rivendel, Cecilia knew that their journey was far from over.

14

CHAPTER 14

The news of Cecilia's return to Rivendel, pregnant with the future heir, rippled through both kingdoms like a storm.

In Rivendel, it was met with a mix of relief and anxiety; their future was tied to the child she carried.

The whispers of war, however, did not dissipate, and the fragile peace between Rivendel and Azmariah hung by a thread.

In Azmariah, King Ferdinand's erratic behavior only grew worse after Cecilia's departure.

The high society of Azmariah, once loyal to their king, now openly questioned his ability to lead.

Their faith in King Ferdinand had been shaken by his reckless decisions, and with Cecilia gone, their hopes for a stable future seemed bleak.

Rumors of rebellion brewed in the shadows, fueled by the king's diminishing grasp on power.

Rivendel was no less troubled.

The noble families, already distrustful of Azmariah, grew increasingly agitated by the threat King Ferdinand posed.

They questioned whether Rivendel could afford to continue its alliance with Azmariah, especially with a ruler as unstable as King Ferdinand.

The council meetings grew more tense, with voices raised in anger and fear.

In the heart of this turmoil, Leo and Cecilia found themselves at a crossroads.

The weight of their kingdoms' futures pressed down on them, and their once-childish squabbles now seemed like distant memories.

They knew that the decisions they made in the coming days would determine not only their fate but the fate of thousands.

A meeting of the highest council was called in Rivendel, with the nobles, military leaders, and advisors gathered to discuss their next move.

The tension in the room was palpable as Leo and Cecilia entered, their presence commanding attention.

Leo took his place at the head of the table, his expression stern.

"We are here to discuss the future of Rivendel and Azmariah. The situation has grown dire, and we must decide how to proceed."

Lord Alaric, one of the most influential nobles, spoke up first.

"Prince Leo, it is clear that King Ferdinand has lost his mind. His demands are outrageous, and his actions have endangered our kingdom.

We must act decisively before he drags us into a war we cannot afford."

A murmur of agreement swept through the room. Cecilia, seated beside Leo, felt a knot tighten in her stomach.

She knew the council's concerns were valid, but the thought of abandoning her father, despite his madness, filled her with dread.

"What do you suggest, Lord Alaric?" Leo asked, his voice measured.

"We must prepare for the worst," Lord Alaric replied.

"If Ferdinand continues to make demands, we should consider severing ties with Azmariah altogether.

Our priority must be to protect Rivendel, even if it means going to war."

Cecilia's heart sank. She had feared this moment, the moment when her loyalty to Rivendel would be tested against her loyalty to her homeland.

She looked to Leo, hoping for some sign of reassurance.

But before Leo could respond, another voice cut through the tension-General Armand, the head of Rivendel's military.

"With all due respect, my lords, severing ties with Azmariah is not so simple. We have a duty to protect our future heir.

Any rash action could jeopardize both Cecilia and the child she carries.

We must find a way to neutralize King Ferdinand without endangering the royal family."

Leo nodded in agreement.

"General Armand is right. We cannot afford to act impulsively.

Our priority is to ensure the safety of Cecilia and our child, as well as the stability of both kingdoms."

The room fell silent as the weight of Leo's words settled over the council.

It was a delicate balance they needed to strike-

one wrong move could plunge both kingdoms into chaos.

Cecilia, gathering her courage, spoke up.

"There may be a way to defuse the situation without resorting to war.

If we can secure the loyalty of Azmariah's nobility, they might support a peaceful resolution.

Ferdinand's power is waning, and we can use that to our advantage."

The council members exchanged glances, considering Cecilia's proposal.

It was a risky strategy, but it offered a glimmer of hope in an otherwise grim situation.

Leo turned to her, his gaze filled with a mix of admiration and concern.

"Are you sure about this, Cecilia? It could be dangerous for you to return to Azmariah, even with the support of some nobles."

Cecilia met his eyes, her resolve unwavering. "I have to do this, Leo.

If there's a chance to avoid bloodshed, I must take it. For our child, and for the future of our kingdoms."

The council agreed to Cecilia's plan, though with great reluctance.

They would send envoys to Azmariah's noble families, gauging their support for a peaceful resolution.

Meanwhile, Cecilia would return to Azmariah under the guise of seeking reconciliation with her father, while secretly rallying the nobility against Ferdinand's rule.

As preparations were made, Leo struggled with his conflicting emotions.

The thought of sending Cecilia back into the lion's den filled him with dread, but he knew there was no other option.

He could see the determination in her eyes, the same strength that had drawn him to her in the first place.

On the eve of Cecilia's departure, Leo found her in the garden, her hands gently resting on her belly.

The moonlight bathed her in a soft glow, and for a moment, all the turmoil seemed to fade away.

"I don't want to let you go," Leo admitted, his voice low and filled with emotion.

Cecilia turned to him, a small smile on her lips.

"I know. But we have to do this, Leo. We have to try and save our kingdoms from tearing each other apart."

He reached out, pulling her close, his hand resting over hers on her belly.

"Promise me you'll be careful. I can't lose you or our child."

She leaned into him, her heart aching at the thought of what lay ahead.

"I promise, Leo. We'll come back to Rivendel, together. And when we do, we'll face whatever comes next-

together."

As they stood there, wrapped in each other's embrace, the storm clouds gathered on the horizon.

The fate of their kingdoms hung in the balance, and the stakes had never been higher.

15

—·—

CHAPTER 15

The news of Cecilia's bold decision to return to Azmariah spread like wildfire across Rivendel.

But amidst the political turmoil and the delicate plans being set into motion, another piece of news captured the kingdom's attention-

the arrival of Queen Isabella, Cecilia's mother, who had been living in seclusion for years.

Queen Isabella was a figure of mystery and grace, known for her wisdom and strength during her reign alongside King Ferdinand.

Her decision to step away from the throne had been sudden, leading many to speculate about the reasons behind her retreat.

But now, with her daughter's future and the fate of both kingdoms at stake, she had returned.

The palace was abuzz with anticipation as the Queen's carriage approached the grand entrance.

Servants lined the hallways, whispering amongst themselves, while guards stood at attention, their expressions solemn.

Cecilia, standing with Leo at the top of the staircase, felt her heart quicken with a mix of excitement and apprehension.

She hadn't seen her mother in years, and the circumstances of her return were anything but ordinary.

As the carriage came to a stop, the doors opened to reveal Queen Isabella, her presence commanding respect and awe.

She stepped out gracefully, her royal gown flowing behind her, and with a simple nod, she acknowledged the assembled crowd.

Her gaze then lifted to meet Cecilia's, and in that moment, all the years of separation melted away.

Cecilia descended the stairs, her emotions a whirlwind as she approached her mother.

The moment they were close enough, Isabella reached out, pulling Cecilia into a warm embrace.

"My dear Cecilia," she whispered, her voice filled with both relief and concern.

"I've missed you so much."

Cecilia held onto her mother, tears welling up in her eyes.

"I've missed you too, Mother. So much has happened...

I didn't know if you would ever return."

Isabella pulled back slightly, cupping Cecilia's face in her hands.

"I returned because you need me. Your father... our kingdom... they're in grave danger.

But we will face it together, my dear. You're not alone."

Leo watched the reunion from a short distance, feeling a sense of respect for the Queen.

He had heard stories of her strength and wisdom, and seeing her now, he understood why she was revered by so many.

As they made their way inside the palace, he knew that Queen Isabella's return would be a turning point in their struggle to secure the future of both kingdoms.

The tension in the air was palpable as Cecilia felt the first pangs of labor.

The Queen, her mother, was by her side, her hands trembling slightly despite her composed demeanor.

Her eyes were locked on Cecilia, filled with a mixture of anxiety and joy at the imminent birth of her grandchild.

It was a momentous occasion, the birth of a new heir, a symbol of unity between two once-warring kingdoms.

Cecilia's breathing grew heavy, her pain evident as she clutched the edges of the bed.

The room was filled with the hushed whispers of the midwives, the occasional clinking of metal tools, and the heavy scent of burning incense intended to calm both mother and child.

The Queen gently brushed Cecilia's hair back, her voice soothing.

"You're doing well, my dear. Soon, this pain will bring forth the greatest joy."

But despite the reassuring words, the Queen's eyes revealed her true feelings-

a deep worry, not just for Cecilia's well-being, but for the future that this child would inherit.

The tension between the kingdoms was at an all-time high, and she knew that this child's birth would only add more pressure on their already fragile peace.

Hours passed, each one feeling like an eternity, until finally, a piercing cry filled the room.

The midwives moved swiftly, cleaning the newborn and wrapping it in soft linens before handing the child to Cecilia.

She gazed down at her baby, tears of relief and joy streaming down her face.

The Queen, too, wept quietly, her hand resting on Cecilia's shoulder.

"A beautiful baby boy," the Queen whispered, her voice thick with emotion.

"A new prince for Rivendel and Azmariah."

But the joy was short-lived. As soon as the baby was settled in Cecilia's arms, the Queen's expression hardened.

She knew there was a message that needed to be delivered, a crucial report to the King.

Leo was supposed to handle it, to bring the news to Cecilia's father, but he was nowhere to be found.

The Queen's eyes narrowed as she called for the palace guards, her voice sharp.

"Where is Prince Leo? He must inform the King at once."

The guards exchanged nervous glances, each one uncertain.

It was unheard of for Leo to be absent at such a critical moment.

Panic began to creep into the room, and the Queen's fear mirrored Cecilia's, who, despite her exhaustion, began to sense that something was terribly wrong.

As the minutes turned into hours, dread filled the palace.

Whispers spread like wildfire-

rumors of betrayal, of abduction, of enemies lurking in the shadows.

The joy of the newborn's arrival was overshadowed by the terror of Leo's disappearance.

In the dead of night, far from the safety of the palace, Leo was bound and blindfolded in a dark, damp chamber.

His head throbbed from the blows he had received during his capture.

He strained against his restraints, his mind racing as he tried to piece together what had happened.

The sound of footsteps echoed through the chamber, and soon, a figure appeared.

It was Wendy, a mercenary known for her ruthlessness and precision.

She approached Leo with a cold, calculating look in her eyes, but there was a flicker of something else-
curiosity.

"You're probably wondering why you're here," Wendy said, her voice a low, mocking drawl.

Leo didn't respond, his eyes narrowing as he studied her.

Wendy stepped closer, her knife glinting in the dim light as she twirled it between her fingers.

"The KING ordered this, you know," she continued, her tone almost casual.

"But I can't help but wonder why. Why would he want his own daughter's husband out of the picture, especially now?"

Leo remained silent, his mind working furiously.

He had known that his father-in-law was a calculating man, but this?

This was beyond anything he had imagined.

Wendy's eyes bore into his, searching for answers.

"You're going to tell me everything, Prince.

Because, honestly, I'm not sure I like the idea of working for a madman."

Leo's lips twitched into a bitter smile.

"The KING is desperate," he said slowly.

"Desperate enough to try and control the future of both kingdoms by any means necessary."

Wendy's expression shifted, her curiosity turning to something more dangerous-interest.

She leaned in closer, her knife stopping its dance.

"Go on."

Leo met her gaze unflinchingly.

"He thinks that by getting rid of me, he can manipulate Cecilia, bend her to his will. But he underestimates her, and me.

Whatever he's planning, it won't work."

Wendy studied him for a moment longer before she straightened up, slipping the knife back into its sheath.

"You're an interesting man, Prince Leo. Too bad your father-in-law doesn't see it that way."

The tension in the room thickened, both of them understanding the gravity of the situation.

Leo knew that his life was hanging by a thread, and Wendy knew that her loyalties were being tested.

Back at the palace, the Queen held Cecilia's hand as they waited for any word of Leo.

The joy of the new prince's birth was overshadowed by fear and uncertainty, and Cecilia's heart ached with the unbearable weight of her husband's absence.

16

CHAPTER 16

The birth of Cecilia and Leo's son brought a brief moment of peace amidst the chaos that engulfed their lives.

Named Leonilia, the child symbolized the union of two kingdoms and carried the hope of a brighter future.

The name, a blend of his parents' names, was a testament to the bond that had formed between them despite the odds.

Cecilia, holding her son in her arms, felt a rare moment of contentment.

But she knew this peace was fragile.

In the days following Leonilia's birth, Wendy, the mercenary who had once been an enemy, became an unexpected ally.

She admired Cecilia's strength and was drawn to Leo's determination.

Wendy had seen firsthand the corruption in Azmariah, and her loyalty shifted.

She now had a vested interest in helping the couple bring down the oppressive forces that had driven their kingdoms to the brink of collapse.

Wendy, with her knowledge of Azmariah's underworld, proved invaluable.

She discreetly gathered information on the high society members who had conspired against Cecilia and Leo.

Their arrogance and greed had led to the downfall of Azmariah, but they remained oblivious, blinded by their wealth and power.

Wendy's plan was simple but effective: expose their corruption and turn the people against them.

She advised Cecilia and Leo to use their influence to spread rumors and leak information about the high society's misdeeds.

The truth, once hidden, began to surface.

The common people, who had suffered under the weight of heavy taxes and endless wars, were enraged.

Protests erupted, and the once powerful nobles found themselves cornered.

Cecilia and Leo watched from a distance as Azmariah's high society began to crumble.

Their downfall was swift and merciless.

The nobles, who had once walked with their heads held high, were now brought to their knees, begging for mercy.

The gods they had long neglected were their last refuge.

The palace, once a symbol of Azmariah's glory, became a haunting reminder of its decline.

The once grand halls were now filled with echoes of despair.

King Ferdinand, who had orchestrated his daughter's marriage for the sake of his kingdom, was a broken man.

He had lost control of his court and his people.

His mind, once sharp and cunning, was clouded with regret and fear.

As the high society crumbled, so did the kingdom's economy.

The gold that once flowed freely through the city's streets was now scarce.

The merchants who had thrived under the nobles' protection were left bankrupt.

The people turned to their gods, praying for salvation, but their prayers went unanswered.

The once proud nobles were stripped of their titles and wealth.

Some fled the kingdom, while others sought refuge in the temples, hoping to appease the gods they had long ignored.

Their humiliation was complete, and their power was shattered.

With Azmariah's high society in ruins, Cecilia and Leo saw an opportunity to rebuild.

Wendy's assistance had been crucial, but now it was up to them to lead their people out of the darkness.

Cecilia, holding Leonilia close, felt a renewed sense of purpose.

She had endured so much for the sake of her kingdom, and now it was time to reclaim what had been lost.

Leo, standing beside her, was no longer the carefree prince she had first met.

He had changed, and so had she.

Their bickering and disagreements had given way to a deeper understanding.

They were no longer just pawns in a political game; they were partners in a battle for their people's future.

As they prepared to face the challenges ahead, they knew the road would be long and difficult.

But they were ready.

With Wendy's help, they had brought down the corrupt forces that had plagued Azmariah.

Now, it was time to build something new, something better for Leonilia and the generations to come.

The fall of Azmariah's high society marked the end of an era, but it also signaled the beginning of a new one.

17

—— ◆ ——

CHAPTER 17

The birth of Leonilia, the firstborn of Cecilia and Leo, shook the very foundations of both kingdoms.

In Rivendel, the celebration of the heir's birth was more than just a moment of joy—

it was a declaration of strength and continuity.

Leonilia, with the combined blood of two powerful kingdoms, represented the future, and with his arrival, the political landscape began to shift rapidly.

As the sun rose over Rivendel, casting its golden light on the kingdom's towers and spires, the nobles and courtiers buzzed with talk of the new heir.

Whispers of Leonilia's potential, the strategic importance of his birth, and the impact on the kingdoms' alliance spread like wildfire through the grand halls.

In a dimly lit chamber of the Rivendel palace, King Ferdinand of Azmariah sat opposite King Armand of Rivendel.

Their faces were shadowed, their eyes betraying the weight of unspoken words.

Between them, a map of the two kingdoms lay unfurled on the table, with lines and markers indicating troop movements, territories, and alliances.

"Leonilia's birth changes everything," King Ferdinand began, his voice tinged with a mix of awe and apprehension.

"He is the future—

our future."

Armand nodded slowly, his expression inscrutable. "Indeed, but we must tread carefully.

The birth of an heir can unite, but it can also divide.

We must ensure that Leonilia's existence strengthens our alliance, not weakens it."

King Ferdinand's eyes narrowed as he looked at the map, his mind racing.

"Azmariah's people are restless. They see Leonilia as a symbol of hope, but also as a threat to our independence.

They fear that Rivendel will use him to tighten its grip on our kingdom."

Armand leaned back in his chair, his fingers steepled as he considered Ferdinand's words.

"The people's fears are not unfounded.

But what they do not realize is that Leonilia is as much a son of Azmariah as he is of Rivendel. His birth has the potential to bring peace and prosperity to both kingdoms—

if we play our cards right."

Ferdinand frowned, his mind wrestling with the complexities of the situation.

"We must be cautious. There are those who would seek to exploit this moment of uncertainty.

The high society of Azmariah is already in turmoil, and if we do not manage this carefully, it could lead to rebellion."

Armand's gaze sharpened, and he leaned forward, his voice low and dangerous.

"You must not forget, Ferdinand, that we have control over Azmariah. Your people may think they are free, but the strings are being pulled from here, in Rivendel.

The birth of Leonilia only solidifies our hold on your kingdom."

King Ferdinand stiffened, a flash of anger in his eyes, but he quickly composed himself.

He knew better than to challenge Armand openly.

The King of Rivendel was a master manipulator, a shadowy puppeteer who had orchestrated much of Azmariah's downfall.

But King Ferdinand also knew that his own survival depended on maintaining this delicate alliance.

"We must ensure that Leonilia is seen as a unifying force, not a tool of subjugation," Ferdinand said carefully.

"The people must believe that his birth is a blessing for both kingdoms."

Armand smiled coldly.

"Leave that to me. We will use this moment to tighten our grip on Azmariah, while giving the appearance of peace and unity.

The high society will crumble under the weight of its own corruption, and when it does, the people will have no choice but to turn to us for salvation."

As the kings plotted and schemed, unaware of the true depth of their manipulations, Cecilia sat in her chambers, cradling her newborn son.

She looked down at Leonilia, his tiny hands grasping at the air, his eyes wide and curious.

She felt a surge of love and protectiveness, but also a deep sense of foreboding.

Cecilia had long suspected that there was more to her marriage to Leo than met the eye.

The political games, the power struggles, and the secrets that lurked in the shadows of the court—

all of it had begun to weigh heavily on her heart.

She knew that Leonilia's birth had set events in motion that were beyond her control, and she feared for what the future held.

A soft knock on the door interrupted her thoughts, and she looked up to see Wendy, the enigmatic mercenary who had become her trusted confidante, enter the room.

Wendy's sharp eyes took in the scene, and she gave a small, approving nod as she approached Cecilia.

"How is the little prince?" Wendy asked, her voice surprisingly gentle.

Cecilia smiled, though it didn't reach her eyes.

"He is healthy, thank the gods.

But I can't help but worry about what his birth means for the kingdom—

for both kingdoms."

Wendy's expression hardened, and she placed a reassuring hand on Cecilia's shoulder.

"You are right to be cautious. There are forces at play that even the kings do not fully understand.

But you are stronger than you know, and with Leonilia by your side, you will find a way to protect him—and the kingdom."

Cecilia looked up at Wendy, her eyes filled with determination. "I will do whatever it takes to ensure Leonilia's future.

But I fear that the path ahead will be fraught with danger."

Wendy nodded, her gaze steady.

"It will be. But you are not alone in this. We will face whatever comes together, and when the time is right, we will strike back at those who seek to use you and your son as pawns in their game."

18

CHAPTER 18

The peaceful facade of Rivendel and Azmariah was shattered when a new threat emerged from the shadows.

As the two kingdoms grappled with the political intricacies of their alliance and the birth of Leonilia, a neighboring kingdom—

unbeknownst to them—

saw an opportunity to seize control of the weakened Azmariah.

Rumors of a rebellion began to circulate, and soon, the whispers turned into cries of war.

The Kingdom of Serenia, long envious of Azmariah's once-great wealth and strategic position, saw the turmoil as a chance to expand its influence.

Serenia's armies gathered at the borders, their eyes set on taking advantage of the instability caused by the ongoing power struggles.

In the grand hall of Rivendel, Cecilia and Leo stood together, their faces etched with worry.

Despite their earlier bickering and the strain on their relationship, the gravity of the situation had united them on purpose.

The sight of their newborn son, Leonilia, sleeping peacefully in his cradle, served as a reminder of what was at stake.

"Leo," Cecilia said, her voice trembling with concern.

"We must act quickly. If Serenia invades now, Azmariah will fall before we can do anything."

Leo, his face grim, nodded.

"We need to consolidate our forces and prepare for the worst. But there's something else we need to address first.

There's been a breach. Our spies have reported that King Ferdinand is in danger."

As if on cue, the doors to the hall burst open, and a breathless messenger entered, his face pale with fear.

"Your Majesties, I bring grave news. King Ferdinand has been assassinated."

Cecilia's heart sank. "What? How could this happen?"

The messenger continued, his voice strained.

"It was done by a spy from Rivendel, someone we trusted. They took advantage of the chaos to strike."

Leo's expression darkened.

"We were betrayed from within. We have to prepare for an invasion and deal with this treachery."

As the news of King Ferdinand's death spread, chaos erupted across Azmariah.

The political vacuum left by the king's assassination sparked unrest, with factions vying for control.

In the midst of this turmoil, Wendy, once a trusted ally, revealed her true allegiances.

As a double agent working for Rivendel, her actions had now come back to haunt her.

In a dimly lit room, Wendy stood before Cecilia and Leo, her face a mask of regret and resolve.

"I've done terrible things, and now I must make amends. I'm ready to face whatever comes."

Cecilia's eyes were filled with tears. "You don't have to do this.

We can find another way."

Wendy shook her head. "No. This is my path. I must atone for my actions.

You need to escape. Serenia's forces are closing in, and you must get Leonilia to safety."

Before Cecilia could respond, the sound of clashing swords and cries of battle reached their ears.

The Serenian forces had begun their assault. Leo grabbed Cecilia's hand, his eyes fierce with determination.

"We have to get out now!" Leo shouted.

"I'll stay here and hold them off. You and Leonilia must escape to Rivendel."

Cecilia resisted, her heart aching at the thought of leaving Leo behind.

"No, Leo. I won't leave you."

Leo's face softened, but his resolve remained unshaken.

"It's the only way. If I fall, you must ensure that Leonilia survives. You have to be strong for him."

Reluctantly, Cecilia took Leonilia and fled, using secret passages and hidden routes to escape the palace.

The sounds of battle grew fainter as she made her way to Rivendel, her mind racing with fear and determination.

Meanwhile, in the heart of Azmariah's capital, Leo fought fiercely against the invading Serenian troops.

His sword moved with deadly precision, but the sheer number of enemies overwhelmed him.

An enemy soldier's blade cut across Leo's side, and he staggered, barely managing to stay on his feet.

The pain was intense, but Leo's will was stronger.

He fought through the agony, determined to protect his kingdom and the future he had fought so hard to build.

But as the battle raged on, it became clear that the odds were against him.

Cecilia's escape was fraught with danger.

Her heart pounded as she approached the safety of Rivendel, the weight of her son and the burden of her decisions heavy on her shoulders.

She finally reached the palace, where the guards, upon recognizing her, ushered her inside.

The tension in Rivendel was palpable.

The news of the invasion and the betrayal of their spy spread quickly, causing panic and confusion among the populace.

Cecilia was ushered into a secure chamber, where she took a moment to catch her breath and tend to Leonilia.

In the midst of the chaos, Cecilia's mind was consumed with the thoughts of Leo.

She knew he was fighting a desperate battle, and the image of him wounded and alone haunted her.

She wished for nothing more than to be by his side, but the danger was too great.

In Azmariah, Leo's condition worsened as the battle continued.

His strength waned, and he was eventually captured by the Serenian forces, who took him as a prisoner.

His fate now rested in the hands of his enemies, and the future of both kingdoms hung in the balance.

As Cecilia looked out over Rivendel, she knew that the true test was only the beginning.

The fight to secure their future and protect their son was far from over.

19

— ◆ —

CHAPTER 19

The world outside was a tapestry of turmoil and strife, but within the heart of the war-torn lands, hope began to take root once more.

As the dust settled, the future of Cecilia, Leo, and their newborn son, Leonilia, became the focal point of a fragile new beginning.

In the aftermath of the battle, Rivendel emerged as a beacon of strength, but its victory came at a high cost.

The king of Rivendel, who had secretly manipulated events from the shadows, was found dead under suspicious circumstances.

The power vacuum left by his death prompted a rapid reorganization of the kingdom's leadership.

Leo, having proven his valor and resilience, was elevated to the throne.

His ascension marked the beginning of a new era for Rivendel, one built on the sacrifices of countless lives and the hope for a brighter future.

As Leo prepared to take on the mantle of king, he faced the daunting task of restoring order to his kingdom and ensuring the stability of the alliance with Azmariah.

His heart ached for Cecilia, who was held captive by Serenia's forces, but his determination to reunite with her and secure their son's future drove him forward.

In the prison of Serenia, Cecilia endured days of confinement.

The once-mighty princess was now a prisoner, her dignity and hope tested by the harsh conditions of her captivity.

Serenia's forces, having captured her in their bid for power, sought to use her as leverage to force Rivendel into submission.

Cecilia's spirit remained unbroken, though the pain of separation from her family weighed heavily on her.

Katrina, the loyal servant, had sacrificed her life defending Cecilia. Her death was a heavy blow to both Cecilia and Leo, marking the cost of their struggle for freedom.

Within the dark confines of her cell, Cecilia's thoughts were consumed by her son and the future she envisioned for him.

Her resolve to survive and return to Leo only grew stronger.

The days dragged on, each one a battle of its own as she clung to the hope that Leo would come for her.

Meanwhile, Leo's ascent to the throne of Rivendel was swift and decisive.

His first act as king was to unite the kingdom in its efforts to rescue Cecilia and protect their future.

His leadership was characterized by a blend of fierce determination and compassionate resolve.

He rallied his forces, determined to bring Cecilia back and restore peace to their fractured lands.

The mission to rescue Cecilia was fraught with danger.

Leo, now a king, led a daring and strategic assault on Serenia's stronghold.

His forces, loyal and battle-hardened, clashed with Serenia's defenders in a fierce and chaotic battle.

The stakes were high, and Leo's resolve was unwavering.

As Leo and his troops breached the prison where Cecilia was held, the sight of her weakened but resolute form gave him a renewed sense of purpose.

The rescue was both a personal and political victory, a testament to the strength of their love and their commitment to their kingdom.

Leo's entrance into the prison was met with a mix of relief and defiance.

Cecilia, despite her ordeal, stood tall as he approached.

Their reunion was bittersweet, marked by the relief of escape and the sorrow of Katrina's death.

"I'm here," Leo said, his voice filled with a mix of tenderness and authority.

"We're getting out of here."

Cecilia's eyes welled with tears as she embraced him.

"I knew you would come.

But Katrina... she gave everything."

Leo nodded solemnly. "Her sacrifice will not be forgotten.

We must honor it by ensuring that this kingdom finds its way to peace."

The journey back to Rivendel was both a physical and emotional trial.

Cecilia, recovering from her captivity, found solace in Leo's presence.

Together, they faced the challenges ahead, determined to rebuild their lives and their kingdom.

Upon their return, the people of Rivendel welcomed them with open arms.

The restoration of peace was not immediate, but Leo's leadership and Cecilia's resilience provided a guiding light for their future.

Their son, Leonilia, symbolized the hope and unity of their kingdoms.

As Leo took his place as the rightful king, he worked tirelessly to consolidate his power and restore stability to both Rivendel and Azmariah.

His reign was marked by efforts to heal the wounds of war, address the needs of his people, and fortify the alliance between the two kingdoms.

Cecilia, now by Leo's side as queen, played a crucial role in this process.

Her experience and wisdom, forged through hardship, became a cornerstone of their efforts to create a lasting peace.

Together, they faced the challenges of governance, always keeping the well-being of their son and their kingdoms at the forefront of their efforts.

The future of Rivendel and Azmariah was now in the hands of the new king and queen.

Their love, tested by adversity, became a beacon of hope for their people.

As they worked to build a prosperous and peaceful era, the legacy of their struggles and triumphs served as a reminder of the strength and resilience required to overcome the greatest of challenges.

Their journey, by trials and tribulations: a testament to the power of perseverance and the enduring hope for a brighter future.

20

EPILOGUE

The palace of Rivendel buzzed with quiet excitement.

The young prince Leonilia, now fifteen, was rapidly approaching the age when he would be expected to step into more prominent roles within the kingdom.

His transformation from a boy into a poised and handsome young man had not gone unnoticed.

Tall and graceful, with striking features inherited from both his parents, Leonilia had grown into a figure of admiration and respect.

One sunny afternoon, the royal family gathered in the gardens for a rare moment of relaxation.

The scene was lively with the presence of Leonilia's younger siblings—

Amara, a spirited twelve-year-old with a quick wit;

Victor, an eleven-year-old with a keen interest in strategy;

and Eliza, a ten-year-old who had already shown signs of remarkable creativity.

Leonilia, despite his emerging responsibilities, still made time for his siblings.

Today, they were engaged in a friendly competition to determine who could come up with the most creative solutions to hypothetical problems posed by their father, Leo.

"Alright, team!" Leo announced with a grin.

"The challenge is to devise a strategy to win over a neighboring kingdom that is reluctant to join our alliance. Who's up for it?"

Leonilia's siblings exchanged eager glances. "We're in!" Amara declared, her eyes sparkling with determination.

Leonilia took his place at the head of the discussion, a natural leader even among his siblings.

"Let's consider our approach carefully. We need to understand their concerns and address them."

Victor, with his thoughtful expression, added, "We could host a grand festival in their honor.

A display of our culture and achievements might win their hearts."

Eliza, ever the creative one, chimed in, "And we could include a showcase of our technological advancements!

People love to see new inventions."

Leo and Cecilia watched with pride as their children interacted.

The camaraderie and quick wit displayed were reminiscent of their own early interactions.

Cecilia leaned over to Leo, a smile tugging at her lips.

"I can't believe how much they've grown. Leonilia is truly becoming a remarkable leader."

Leo chuckled, his eyes twinkling with affection.

"Yes, and it seems he's inherited your strategic mind and my sense of humor. Look at how easily he deals with his siblings!"

Leonilia's plan was not just about winning over the neighboring kingdom; it was about bringing his siblings closer together through shared experiences.

As they debated and joked, the garden echoed with laughter and light-hearted bickering.

Later that evening, as the sun dipped below the horizon, the family gathered for dinner.

The atmosphere was filled with warmth and playful banter.

"So, what's the latest on the 'great strategy' of the day?" Cecilia asked, her eyes twinkling with curiosity.

Victor grinned, "Leonilia suggested a festival, and Eliza wants to showcase new inventions.

We've also decided to include a talent show!"

"Ah, a talent show," Leo mused.

"Sounds like fun. Just don't expect me to perform a magic trick."

Leonilia laughed, "Don't worry, Father. I'm sure your talent for telling jokes will be more than enough."

The siblings laughed, and Amara nudged Leonilia.

"You better make sure you have a good plan for the festival, or we might have to put on a show ourselves!"

Leonilia playfully rolled his eyes.

"Don't worry, I've got it all covered. And I'm sure we'll make a great impression."

As the evening wore on, the family continued to enjoy their time together.

The children's laughter and playful arguments filled the palace with a sense of joy that made the burdens of leadership seem distant.

Cecilia and Leo exchanged a look of deep satisfaction.

"Our children are growing up so well," Cecilia said softly. "They're becoming leaders in their own right."

Leo nodded, "Yes, and I'm proud of the person Leonilia is becoming. He's everything we could have hoped for and more."

As the night drew to a close, Leonilia and his siblings gathered in their rooms, their laughter still echoing through the halls.

The future of Rivendel and Azmariah seemed bright, not only because of the strength of their rulers but also due to the promising legacy embodied by their children.

Leonilia lay in bed, his mind already working on new strategies and ideas.

He knew the path ahead would be challenging, but with his family by his side and the lessons learned from his parents, he felt ready to face whatever came next.

With a final glance at the stars outside his window, Leonilia drifted into peaceful slumber, content in the knowledge that he was prepared to carry the legacy of unity and strength that had been well-earned by his parents.